For Pepper+Dahlia.

Enjoy!

Fly Away HOME

and other Caribbean stories

Andy Mead

Illustrated by Kojovi Dawes

LMH Publishing Limited

Consultant Executive Editor: Julia Tan

Copy Editor: Julia Tan

Book Design: Julia-Mei Tan (Singapore)

Cover Design: Susan Lee-Quee

Illustrations: Kojovi Dawes

Layout & Typesetting: Michelle M.A. Mitchell

Published by LMH Publishing Limited
7 Norman Road,
LOJ Industrial Complex
Building 10
Kingston C.S.O., Jamaica
Tel: 876-938-0005; 938-0712
Fax: 876-759-8752
Email: lmhbookpublishing@cwjamaica.com
Website: www.lmhpublishingjamaica.com

Printed in the U.S.A.   ISBN 976-8184-41-8

Contents

Fly Away Home

Berris didn't go to school. No school could keep him. When he was younger he sometimes went to school; some days he was just there. The teacher would look round from the blackboard to find that Berris had appeared, as if from nowhere, and was sitting near the front, a serious solemn look on his face. It was just as likely that when she turned her back again, he'd disappear. It didn't matter whether Berris was there or not really; he wasn't any trouble. He never did or said anything at school. He wasn't stupid, far from it, but he never said a word. The only sound he ever made was to laugh, but he laughed really quietly and his whole face would laugh. His eyes, his cheeks and his mouth, would crease and stretch into a look of pure pleasure and delight and make everyone else laugh too. But then the laugh would die away, the serious solemn look would return, and his eyes would have this far away look, so you sometimes never knew whether he recognised you or not, even if he was looking right at you. Now, Berris didn't go to school at all. No one was quite sure how old he was, but it was assumed he was too old to have to go to school, which saved anyone the bother of having to make sure he did.

Until he was six, Berris lived with his mother and was a normal, happy little boy, always talking, laughing and playing with other children. But just before his seventh birthday, his mother died and Berris disappeared. They went to bed one night, and the next morning a neighbour, noticing no movement from the house, went in and found Berris's mother dead in the bed, and Berris gone. The autopsy said she'd had a heart defect which had gone unnoticed. Then, three days after the funeral, Berris appeared again, sitting on the steps of his mother's house. After that he went to live with his father and grandfather but from that day on, he never said a word. I heard all this from the sweetie man who knew everything about everyone.

I got to know Berris better, because his grandfather came to cut the grass for us. We didn't have a lawn mower; if your grass got too long you cut it with a machete. Berris's granddad came and did it for us. He was a tall, proud man with a long bushy beard and long hair like a Rasta. Many people were scared of him, and he did look fairly fearsome, but really he was the kindest, gentlest man you could meet. He did everything with the minimum of effort. He walked quite quickly, but his feet barely left the ground and when he chopped the grass he would take off his shirt, lean on a stick with his left hand and swing the machete in long easy swathes with his right. The muscles in his back were knotted and hard, glistening with sweat. He talked in a

2

slow measured way, as though he was thinking carefully about everything he said before he said it. Everybody called him Brother John. He must have had a surname, but I never heard anyone use it.

Berris would come with his grandfather sometimes, and when he did, we would leave whatever we were doing and go off into the fields or down to the river with him. He taught us how to swim like Tarzan, fight like Ninjas and hunt like Indians. He taught us how to make radios out of matchboxes by making holes in the front to let the sound out, carefully drawing in control knobs with a pencil, and sticking a grass stalk down the side for an aerial. Then you had to catch a wasp to put inside it, so that every time you shook the box the wasp would start buzzing, and it sounded like static on the radio.

The more I knew Berris, the more he amazed me. He was so clever. Everything he did always worked, and as I spent more and more time with him, I began to find out things about him that others didn't know. For a start, I found out that he could talk. He spoke quietly, and never wasted his words. He never made exclamations or asked questions; he only said what was necessary. The day I first heard him speak was a bit of a shock, not only because I'd never heard him speak before but because of what he told me. We were sitting in the shade of some guava trees by the river, and Berris was sharpening thin bamboo sticks to make traps for birds. I was idly flicking little off-cuts of bamboo into the water and watching them drift away downstream, when in a very soft, far away voice he said, "Me father dead this week."

I was so surprised to hear him speak, I stopped mid flick and just stared at him. He looked at me with that sad, solemn expression, and I tried to regain my composure and answer him as well as I could. I couldn't think of anything better to say than, "How come?"

"Him drown," he said in that same far away voice; "de big turtle kill him."

"How you mean, de big turtle kill him?" I asked lamely. "Turtle can't kill nobody."

He didn't say anything for a while; he just kept cutting the bamboo with short clean flicks of his machete, then he stopped, looked up, and for a few seconds stared ahead of him with that curious distant look in his eyes.

"Him want to kill dat big turtle," he said softly. "But dat turtle going to kill him first."

I didn't understand but I didn't say so. I thought about Berris's father. He was a tall man with the same face as Berris and that same vague distant look in his eyes. I'd seen him last Saturday standing waist deep in the water by his canoe, selling red mullet strung through the gills on lengths of palm leaf. His canoe was called Independence and it was long and slender with the black, green and gold of Jamaica painted round it. It didn't seem possible that he could now be dead. The unfamiliar sound of Berris's soft voice broke into my thoughts.

"Him go fishing last Tuesday," he said, "and him don't come back yet."

I did a silent calculation. Today was Saturday. That meant four days, five if you counted today.

"Maybe him gone to Black River or Bluefields or ......," my voice tailed off.

I couldn't really cope with this, but Berris seemed unconcerned. He went back to cutting his sticks while I tried desperately to think of something to say.

"How you know him dead?" was all I managed to come up with. Once again there was a long silence before Berris stopped cutting sticks and looked up.

"Listen Jobe, before me mada dead me did know. When she lay down on the bed, I did know that she will never get up again. So me run, because me never wan' dead as

4

well. Last week me faada tell me that him going to shoot the big turtle and kill him." He paused, "Brother John tell me this same thing like you. Him say, 'Don't worry Berris, him soon come', but I know him not coming back."

As he said these last few words, he looked away into the distance and closed his eyes. His lips moved silently, as if he was praying, and I gave up trying to think of anything more to say.

On Monday at school I saw Johnny Gopal outside the canteen at break time,

"Hey Jobe," he shouted across the crowd of starving third years, "you hear 'bout George Bedford?"

"Who?" I shouted back.

"George Bedford. You know, Berris's father."

"Dem find im?" I asked.

Across the canteen, Johnny nodded, and I could read the rest in his face. He pushed his way through the hungry crowds towards me.

"Zebby Williams' father catch a big turtle in im net, and when im pull de net out of de water im pull up George Bedford body. It looked like George shoot de turtle, get all tangled up in the line on the spear, and de turtle pull im down and drown im."

Johnny's voice carried on describing the body, and the crowds who had gathered round Dave Williams' boat, but I didn't really hear any of it. In fact I didn't hear anything. It was as if I'd entered a soundproof, glass box which allowed me to still be surrounded by people, who I could see were laughing, talking and joking, but I couldn't hear anything. Deep inside my head, I could hear Berris's voice saying quietly over and over again, "de turtle a go kill im first." Gradually, the glass box melted away, and I heard Johnny's voice again filtering through into my consciousness. "......and Zebby say de body all swell up with de water and the skin all tight and shiny like shoes

5

leather." He looked at me with a grimace of disgust on his face. "You see Berris?" I asked him.

"No. Dat is another thing. Nobody see Berris at all since Sunday morning. 'im gone!" That figures, I thought to myself; in fact nobody saw Berris for a week. Brother John told me that he'd come back when he came to cut the grass, but Berris wasn't with him. I didn't see him again for about three months. There was no rain, the grass didn't get very high, so Brother John didn't come, and thoughts of Berris and his father faded, until early one morning in July at the beginning of the summer holidays.

I was down by the river fishing. There wasn't much river left now. In the dry season, it almost disappeared except for the big, deep pools which ended up full of fish. Fishing was easy; you didn't even need bait. As soon as you threw the line in, and pulled it slowly out again, there'd be a fish on the end of it. We never ate these fish; the idea was to see how many you could catch, keep them in a kerosene tin and then throw them back in again. I'd been by the river for about an hour and I had a tin full. As I was contemplating tipping them all back in and going home, Berris came cycling down the lane on a rusty old bike with a huge black box on the back. He saw me and slowed down, then he steered the bike in under the trees and stopped.

"What happen Berris?" I greeted him, "I don't see you fe a long time, you alright?"

Berris didn't answer; he just nodded and grinned. He got off the bike, leaned it up against the tree, and still without a word, unlocked the black box on the back with a key that was attached to a string round his neck. He motioned to me to come and look. I tipped the tin of fish back into the pool, and ran over to the bike. In the black box were a dozen or so old machetes. Their wooden handles were smooth and dark with wear and sweat, and they had been

6

file sharpened so many times there was hardly any blade left. They looked like very short, sharp daggers.

"What you going to do with dem Berris?" I asked.

Berris looked at me, still grinning. "Sell dem." He said quietly.

I laughed. "Who going to buy dem? Dem don't worth nothing."

He reached into the box and from under the pile of machetes; he pulled out a piece of cardboard. On it, in red paint, were the words,

NATIV WEAPONS $5

"Americans," he said, "down Bluefields beach. You want come?"

He put the sign back, shut and locked the lid of the box, while I hid my kerosene tin in the bushes. Ten minutes later, we were out of town and heading towards Bluefields. I was sitting on the crossbar, and Berris pedalled strongly and smoothly; neither of us spoke. I was remembering the last time Berris went to Bluefields to sell things to tourists. He had walked, pushing a home-made cart full of little cages, and in each cage was a mongoose. He'd sold them for $5 each, and the Yanks had fallen over each other to buy them. I couldn't believe it. As soon as they go to Customs at the airport, they'd be confiscated, but they still bought them. Crazy people, but like Berris had said at the time, "American tourist don't got no sense, dem will buy anyting."

When we got to Bluefields, Berris leaned his bike under the trees, opened up the box, and waited for customers. I went off swimming for a while, and when I came back about an hour later, Berris was standing silently, watching an extremely fat American tourist showing his ever fatter wife, one of the machetes.

7

"Just think Honey," he was saying, "This knife was used to kill a lion. Now ain't that something?"

His wife was nodding enthusiastically and making little squealing noises of delight.

"Gee Honey, it's so exciting I can't wait to tell Marge and the girls."

"I can't wait to show it to the guys at work, and so cheap, only $5."

Berris stood motionless, his face solemn and serious. I stood behind the two tourists, trying very hard not to laugh out loud. I looked at Berris and he winked at me, but his face never cracked.

He took the $5 bill, and with a subservient nod of his head said, "Tank you sah, God Bless you sah," and the fat pair waddled off ecstatic.

I couldn't hold the laughter any longer, and I doubled up and could hardly speak.

"You really tell him dat somebody use dat knife to kill a lion?" I spluttered.

Berris smiled, "Yeah" he said quietly. "You can tell American anything at all, and dem will believe you."

"How much you sell?" I asked, peering into the box.

"Four," he answered. "Dat will do fe today. Come, we go buy some patty and cocobread."

We made our way slowly back towards the town. We stopped at a shop and bought some food, which we ate sitting under the trees at the top of Pelican Hill, looking out across the sea which sparkled and dazzled in the afternoon sun. It was a perfect Saturday. Berris sat with his back to a palm tree, looking out to sea. His face was calm and thoughtful, and we ate in silence. When he'd finished his food, Berris leaned forward, and picking up a stick began to scratch some marks in the dust at his feet. I leaned forward to look at what he was writing. In large, neat print he had scratched the number 18.

"Why you write dat?" I asked.

Berris took a long time to answer. He idly flicked his hand in the dust and the number disappeared.

"Because tomorrow is my birthday, the 12th July. I will be eighteen years old, and 18 is my number."

"How you mean, 18 is your number?" I asked as I didn't understand.

"Come here Jobe," said Berris, "Give me you hand."

He took my right hand in both his, turned the palm up towards him, and looked intently at it. He held it gently and began to trace lines with his fingers, whispering quietly to himself. Finally he let go of my hand and leaned back against the tree, his eyes shut, his lips moving silently as if he was praying. Then he leaned forward and put his face close to mine.

"Listen Jobe," he said in a hushed voice, "Brother John uncle, who live up in the bush, back of Negril, tell me dis. When you born, God write a number in you hand. Dat number is how long you will live. Most people can't see it, but some people like me can read de number. Me see de number in me mada hand, and in me faada han'. Dat is why me did know dat dem going to dead soon. First of all me couldn't see no number in my hand but now me can see it, 18."

I stared at Berris in disbelief. I had hoped he was joking, but from the tone of his voice and the look on his face, I knew he wasn't.

"What number you read in my hand?" I asked hesitantly. I didn't want to hear the answer, but I had to ask the question. Once again, he took a long time to answer.

"You number not too clear Jobe," he said quietly. "But is a big number so don't worry."

Relief flooded through me like the first breath you take when you come up from a dive.

"You sure about your number, Berris?" I asked. "Maybe you don't read it right, maybe it say 81."

I tried to sound light-hearted and optimistic but Berris shook his head.

"No mistake Jobe," he said. "But don't worry, Brother John number say 50, but him long past 50 now, so it don't always work out. Anyway, me no 'fraid, Me can dead anytime, you know what the song say, 'One bright morning when my work is over, I will fly away home.' Everybody have fe dead sometime."

Berris picked up the stick he'd been scratching with and threw it out over the wall that marked the edge of the cliff. It cartwheeled away, out of sight, down towards the sea below, and we watched it in silence. Neither of us mentioned the subject again. The days went past, turned quickly into weeks, and before I had time to talk to Berris seriously again, we were back at school and I hardly saw him at all.

Christmas came and went, and still I didn't see Berris. Brother John told me he was fine. He had a job working for a rich doctor who lived up at Frome near the sugar factory, and sometimes he stayed with an aunt in Grange Hill when he was working late. By the time the summer had come round again, I had almost forgotten about Berris's number, and I hadn't seen him to talk to for almost a year.

The day after we broke up, I was standing by the school gate with Boysie and Errol. They stayed with us during term time because they lived so far away from school, but now they were waiting for the minibus that would take them home to their families for the summer holidays. A truck rumbled in our direction, travelling towards the market in the town. It was over-loaded, and the back was swaying alarmingly from side to side. It took the left-hand bend very wide. As it disappeared round the corner, I heard a scream, which sent a prickle of fear down my neck, and a riderless bicycle rolled into view and toppled over in the middle of the road. The screaming turned to sobbing and a woman's voice was crying, "Lord have mercy, de bwoy dead, him dead, him dead."

Everything seemed to slow down. I got that feeling again. I was in an invisible box, seeing everything but not hearing anything; this time, everything was happening in slow motion. I recognised the bicycle. The black box on the back had fallen open, and the contents spilled all over the road. There was a machete, a file, and a tin Thermos flask that rolled silently across the road and into the gutter. Errol and Boysie began to run towards the voice round the corner, but I was rooted to the spot. It was the 12th July and in my head Berris's voice kept repeating over and over again, "One bright morning, when my work is over, I will fly away home."

Cricket Lovely Cricket

R icky lived for cricket. He played from morning till night, and would have played all night if there had been anyone left to play with him. The rest of us had some brains; we packed up when the light was so bad it was dangerous. Ricky would plead with us to stay out.

"One more over," he would beg. "You can still see de ball. It not dark yet."

But one by one, the players left the yard. Bags were picked up, bicycles retrieved from the hedge, and as the crickets began their night-long choir practice, weary legs and arms, bruised and battered by the afternoon's exertions dragged themselves off to bed. Ricky was always the last. He would stay until the last one went in, which was usually me, as it was our yard we played in.

When he realised that there was no one else to play with, he would reluctantly pick up his ancient bike and pedal slowly off, in the direction of home. As he rode off he always said the same thing, "See you tomorrow Jobe. Get first a' pick tomorrow den you can pick me first."

Pick Ricky first? Nobody picked Ricky first! The pickers were usually me, because it was my yard we were playing in, and Maxie, because he had the bat. The bat was sacred. It was the only real bat that any of us had ever had. Maxie's uncle, who played cricket for a local side had given it to him because it had a big split in it, and as they had got a bit of sponsorship that season he had bought a new one. Maxie bandaged the bat carefully. He oiled it up, and brought it to school one morning wrapped in an old sheet. He still had the sheet, and still wrapped it up every night and took it home. Our other bat was just a big bit of wood, with one end chopped a bit thinner so you could get your hands round it. We called it 'The Channer'. Don't ask me why, and it weighed a ton.

Anyway, as I was saying, Ricky never got picked first. Despite all his keenness, enthusiasm and bravery in the face of fire, Ricky was absolutely useless. The trouble with Ricky was that he wanted to do everything too fast. He did everything at 100 miles per hour. He spoke so fast it was difficult to understand him. He ran everywhere, and I always felt that it was just plain wickedness keeping a kid like him in a classroom all day because he just couldn't keep still. I think quite a number of the teachers agreed with me because they were always sending him out to stand in the sun. Ricky must have spent hours standing outside various classrooms, hopping from one leg to the other like a little bird. He never seemed to mind, never

13

bore a grudge, never complained. He just accepted it as part of his life. If he was sent out of a classroom and had to stand in a corridor, or on a landing where nobody could see him, he would do things to amuse himself, like press-ups or chin-ups on the doorframes. On one occasion, he was actually caught hanging by his fingertips over the stairwell. He wasn't going to jump; he was just hanging there to see what it was like.

He played cricket like that. When he tried to bowl, the ball went everywhere but towards the wicket. When he batted, he lashed out at everything, and usually lasted about three balls before the ball either accidentally hit his bat and went up in the air and he was caught, or his wickets were flattened as he lashed wildly at the air. When he was fielding he was always in the wrong place. He kept moving, changing position, running round, to where the ball had been hit last time, and you could guarantee that every time he moved, the next ball would be hit in the air to the place where he'd been last. Not surprisingly he was always the last one to be picked. In fact, Ricky was never picked at all. He was always the kid that one team or the other got stuck with, and it was usually me.

He was a good kid though; everybody really liked him, but when you were playing serious cricket, you could not afford to have someone useless on your side. We played every weekday after school in our front yard. It was quite a good wicket, but we had to use the road, the field across the road, and the adjacent pasture, which was a bit overgrown and had a ditch running across it. The fielders had to cross a few fences to get into position, but it made it more interesting.

Our house was right next door to school and every afternoon at half past three, an untidy group of about a dozen second years would gather in the middle of the wicket for the toss, the crucial moment of the day. It got dark at about six o'clock every night, being tropical, so if you had to bat second you could end up finishing your innings in darkness. This could seriously damage your chances of winning, or even surviving, given the state of the wicket and the quality of our bowling.

'Bowling' may not be the best way to describe what we did. A series of alternative verbs come to mind. Hurling, chucking, flinging and just plain throwing, to mention but a few. We all knew roughly how to bowl, from watching other people, but none of us had been taught properly, and anyway it went faster if you just threw it. Wes Hall and Charlie Griffiths were our heroes. We'd seen them in real life and spent hours listening to crackly commentaries from around the world, as Wes and Charlie terrorised batsmen.

To play cricket with us, you either had to be very brave or incredibly stupid, and I suppose most of us were a mixture of both. We'd pick sides on Monday, which would stay the same until Friday, and during the week we would play a series of five tests. The sides were pretty evenly matched and the games were quite close, provided of course you could get the first side to bat out, in time for the second side to bat before darkness fell, and that you didn't have Ricky on your side. Ricky was the player who could turn the game for you.

Unfortunately, it was usually the wrong way. He was the sort of player who helped your side snatch defeat from the jaws of victory. He dropped catches, bowled countless wides; you name it, he did it. But he was always apologetic.

"Sorry guys," he would say dolefully. "I'll be better next time."

He never made excuses. He always admitted his weaknesses, and I suppose this was why almost everyone liked him and we still let him play. We all believed, and so did he, that he would only get better, basically because he couldn't get any worse.

Unfortunately, however, not everyone liked him. Maxie and this other kid Clifford, didn't like Ricky at all. He irritated them. It was alright if he was on the other side and they didn't have to suffer from his incompetence. But the laws of chance meant that at least half the time he ended up on their team, and I suppose, because he knew they were watching his every move and commenting loudly on his every slip, Ricky became worse. They weren't really horrible kids, but Maxie was a bit of a perfectionist. He was good at everything he did, and to have one of his side run him out when he was well on his way to a fifty, understandably annoyed him. Clifford was just arrogant. He was nowhere near as good as Maxie but he thought he was, and because his dad was a policeman he had the idea that everyone ought to be respectful to him. Some of the other boys were, but Ricky and I just laughed at him. We weren't unkind but he didn't like it.

He took it from me but not from Ricky.

I started to come under a bit of pressure from Clifford and Maxie to get rid of Ricky.

"Tell him you don't want him in your yard," demanded Clifford. "Tell him your mother say she don't want him break her window."

"Nah!" I lamely stuck up for Ricky. "Let de boy play, just cos you don't like him."

"But him worthless Jobe. Him can't play cricket, and we don't want him no more," said Maxie bluntly.

"Even you have to admit it, him no good fe nuttin' at all."

I didn't know what to say. It was true, he was worthless and he had, in the past, completely ruined some finely balanced and exciting games, by doing something stupid. But I liked Ricky; I liked his happy trusting nature, his openness and complete lack of any malice or unkindness. I admired the way he took everything in his stride and never complained. He wasn't much good at cricket, but he was brilliant at being a human being.

"Just give him one more chance," I pleaded. "Mek him play next week, alright? Him might do something good next week." I was being rather optimistic but I tried to get a bit of conviction into my voice. "Him can play on my side next week, alright? And if we beat you, him can stay. Yeah?"

"Yeah, alright." said Maxie reluctantly. "Him got one more week, cause we are going to win next week for sure."

"Yeah." said Clifford. "Next week is the last time Ricky play cricket wid us. I will make sure of dat."

I didn't say anything to Ricky about my conversation with Clifford and Maxie. On Monday after school we picked sides and for a bit of security I picked Johnny Gopal first. He was a good player to have, as he was the only one of us who could bowl properly. He had been taught by his older brothers to bowl spinners. Not brilliant spinners, but he could get the ball to turn a bit and most of us, who were used to the ball coming at us at eighty miles an hour, didn't know what to do with slow ones, and got ourselves out. He could bat as well, almost as well as Maxie, but the best thing about Johnny was that we had this understanding and batted well together. We really enjoyed playing on the same side. The sides seemed evenly matched, except that we had Ricky, but I had recommended him and so I couldn't complain. Anyway, I was optimistic; this week might be different.

We didn't start well. We lost the toss on Monday and Tuesday, ended up batting in the semi-darkness and lost both games. I felt pressured. I had a weight on my shoulders. I still hadn't told Ricky what Clifford and Maxie had said. We were the only three people who knew how important this set of games were to Ricky's future as a backyard cricketer. Clifford started very aggressively; he was bowling extremely fast and aiming at people's heads. He didn't say anything; he just kept looking at me and Ricky with this knowing smirk on his face. After the second defeat, I could stand it no longer; I had to tell Ricky. I had my chance at school the next day. I was sitting with him in the canteen at lunchtime and most of the others had gone. Ricky didn't have much for lunch; one patty was all he could afford. He was really poor, Ricky. His dad had been killed by a tractor when he was a baby and he only had his mum. She earned what she could by washing people's clothes, but as most people who lived nearby were as poor as she was, she didn't earn much. They ate what she could grow on her little piece of land behind their two-room house right out in the bush, and Ricky was always hungry.

As I told Ricky what Clifford and Maxie had said, I was amazed at the look on his face. I had expected him to be upset or even angry, but as I spoke, he stopped chewing his patty and looked at me open-mouthed.

"Who say dat?" he asked incredulously. "Clifford and Maxie?"

I tried to explain, to make excuses, but Ricky just waved his hand dismissively at me and said, "Don't worry Jobe, you think I care what dem say 'bout me? Them can say what dem want. They think Ricky worthless? I will show them who worthless. I did tell you I will play good one day. Well, I going to play good now Jobe, me and you."

With that he stood up, pushed the bench back hard against the wall, stuffed the rest of the patty in his mouth and jumping across the table, disappeared out the door.

I don't know if it was the relief of having told Ricky, or the boost of enthusiasm he had given me by his determination to play well, but we won the next two games. They were close, but we won with daylight to spare, and at the close of play on Thursday evening, it was all square, two games all. True to his word, Ricky had made a real effort. He had kept a low profile, not done anything really spectacular but at the same time neither had he done anything really stupid.

Clifford had begun to get a bit annoyed, and when Johnny hit him over the road for six to win the game on Thursday, he was not at all happy.

"You watch your head tomorrow Johnny Gopal;" he spat angrily. "You won't get no runs tomorrow, cause I'm going to lick out your pins first ball."

Johnny just laughed, so did Ricky. "Dat's all right Clifford," Ricky shouted after him as he stalked off down the road. "You do what you want tomorrow, I will show you who can't play cricket."

For a moment Clifford didn't answer; he just carried on walking. Suddenly he stopped, turned and pointing at Ricky he said, "You won't have to bother come back next week Ricky , cos you going to be dead."

Ricky let out a loud derisory hoot of laughter, picked up his bike and pedalled off in the opposite direction to Clifford, still laughing.

"He won't laugh tomorrow," muttered Clifford darkly. "Nobody goin' laugh tomorrow."

I didn't know what to say so I went in. I needed to be ready for tomorrow.

Friday, the last game. I was nervous and so was Johnny. Clifford wasn't going to give anyone an inch today. To make it worse, we won the toss. I put Ricky and Patrick in first, partly to get Ricky out of the way early on, (though I didn't tell him that) and partly because I didn't want a fresh Clifford throwing the ball at Johnny's head. Anyway, Ricky had volunteered to go in first. He was calm; in fact I'd never seen him look so confident and relaxed. He stood holding 'The Channer' out in front of him, his thin shoulders slightly hunched. 'The Channer' looked huge in his hands. Clifford, who still had not said much, charged in to bowl. He grunted as he let go of the ball, and it flew like a small cannonball straight towards Ricky's head. Ricky ducked, stuck 'The Channer' hopefully in the air, the ball hit it and sailed right over the roof of the house behind, and on to the tennis courts. Six runs. The rest of us on the batting side laughed till we cried. We rolled around holding our stomachs, and quite a few of the fielders did the same. Clifford was incensed; he came hurtling in again, and the ball, a bit lower this time was hit by Ricky, straight back over his head for four.

"Lick him Ricky, lick him hard," shouted Johnny. Ricky didn't answer; he just stood there, with 'The Channer' on his shoulder like a baseball bat, waiting for the next ball. In came Clifford again, and once again Ricky just lazily swung 'The Channer'and the ball hit the top edge and curled away over the house again for six. What a start, sixteen runs off three balls! We were jubilant. We sang and jeered and laughed, and Clifford got angrier and angrier. The trouble was, the angrier he got the less accurate he became, and the ball flew around all over the place. Ricky stayed there, ducking and bobbing and sticking 'The Channer' out hopefully at every ball that was hurled at him. He was eventually caught going for a big hit having made thirty-two, most of them off Clifford's bowling. The rest of us made another forty between us, and we were all out for seventy-two. Ricky had played his best innings ever, but Clifford and Maxie were not impressed. "Dis game don't finish yet," Clifford snarled as we changed over. "We goin' to kill you now."

Their opening batsman made a good start, and the score began to creep slowly up. We got a few wickets but they were gradually gaining on us. With only one wicket left, they needed twenty to win, and Clifford and Maxie were together. It was beginning to turn dusk but they had plenty of time to score runs. They were both batting really cautiously now as it began to get darker, slowly picking off the runs till they only needed another four to win. This would definitely be the last over we could safely bowl and it had to be good. I took the ball and walked out onto the road. As I turned, I thought at least Ricky had shown them he wasn't that useless, even if we were going to lose. Maybe they'd still let him play. Clifford's voice broke into my thoughts.

"Bowl up Jobe, you're going to lose. Make haste, bowl so I can lick off dese runs."

The sneer in his voice galvanised me into action. I ran in and bowled. It was a short one that reared up, and Clifford, trying to avoid the ball in the face, swung across the line, got the top edge and the ball went high in the air, over the fence to where Ricky was fielding in the long grass. Ricky looked up and began to move backwards, hands cupped in front of his chest as the ball, reaching the top of its flight began to fall back towards him. We all had our eyes on the ball; even Clifford and Maxie stood still. If Ricky caught it, we would win; if he dropped it, it would be four runs and we would lose. Ricky kept going back, his eyes on the ball as it came closer and closer, when suddenly, as if by magic, he disappeared.

We all stood gaping in utter amazement. Ricky had vanished into thin air, gone!

After what seemed like half an hour, but can only have been a matter of seconds, we all leapt over or through the fence and ran towards the spot where Ricky had disappeared. Maxie and I got there first, and there was Ricky, lying on his back in the ditch, covered from head to foot in stinking black slime; and in his hands, which were clutched tight to his chest, was the ball.

"Me ketch him!" he said, and began to laugh.

Then we all started. We laughed till the tears ran down our faces and our stomachs hurt, all of us, even Maxie. Well, not quite all of us. Clifford had gone. One minute he was there standing on the edge of the ditch looking in disbelief at Ricky, and the next minute he was gone. He never came back and nobody missed him much.

Cricket – it's a good game; you really can have so much fun and laughter. Well, we certainly did!

Little Pieces of Glass

When we were ten, we had two passions in our lives. Climbing trees and playing marbles. I suppose most people are the same, but all I can remember clearly about junior school is playtime. Life was playtime. We spent hours, crouching in the dust, firing little glass balls into a crudely drawn ring, swinging wildly from branch to branch, through trees whose boughs were obviously made for climbing. God made the world for us to play in. The trees were our climbing frames and our schoolyard was a dustbowl, where little glass fortunes were bitter. Hopes and dreams were often shattered and revenge was always sweet.

There was a fair bit of animosity between our little gang and the bigger boys. It was usually contained, but on occasions it was hard to keep your temper when the big kids used their size as superiority of strength to outplay and outwit you. The little ones kept out of the way; none of them dared interfere or run off and tell.

It was all caused by Audley White. His younger brother, Patrick, was one of our friends, which increased his hatred of us because he and his brother didn't get on at all. Their dad, George White, was a violent man, a legend in our part of the world. He owned a garage and had a temper like a volcano. There were these stories that went around about things he had done to people. One story, which despite being utterly fantastic, we all believed, was that George had dragged an employee from the cab of one of his breakdown trucks, pulled one of his eyes out on its stalk and let it go so that it pinged back into the socket, like a pickled onion on a piece of elastic. He did this because the unfortunate driver had scraped the paintwork of his new truck, trying to back it out of the yard.

Audley lived with his dad, and the dad's girlfriend, or wife. Nobody really knew, while Patrick lived with his mother, George's ex-wife, and there was no love lost between the two camps. Most of the time we played together quite happily, but Audley's bullying and aggression would often spark off bitter arguments, and insults were hurled across at each other. It wasn't worth getting into fights because he was bigger and stronger than all of us.

We were playing marbles one day, just minding our own business, when Audley, who had either lost all his marbles, or left them at home, sauntered over to us, hands in his pockets, looking bored.

"Yuh want we go climb tree?" he suggested.
The rest of us, who were always eager to demonstrate our acrobatic skills on the climbing tree agreed, and gave our

marbles to younger brothers and sisters to hold, or hid them in our own secret places under the school hut, or in the hollow of the logwood trees. I had a special place for mine. The outside pipe, which we used to drink from, had a concrete slab around it and at the back I had hollowed out a hole between the base of the slab and the surrounding earth. This was concealed by a small lump of concrete that had broken away from the rest, and sat neatly on the top of the hole. A perfect hiding place that only I knew about, or so I thought.

We spent the rest of the lunch hour climbing to the top of the tree, and by a series of acrobatic leaps, swings and somersaults, making our way down to the ground, to rejoin the queue for scaling the tree again. The idea was to get to the ground as quickly and as spectacularly as possible, while using the least number of branches. Being smaller, we were lighter and more agile than the bigger ones. We were better than them, and they knew it. After a while, they got fed up with trying to compete, and wandered off, while we carried on being more and more daring, till the bell that signalled the end of lunch hour rang, and we collected up our marbles, and went back in.

I ran to the outside pipe, and pushed my hand into the hole at the back. It was empty; not even one marble was left. I ran quickly and joined the others. I didn't say anything; I couldn't; Miss. Miller was standing at the top of the steps looking grim. She always looked grim. I sat for an hour, copying the sums from the board, and the answers from Patrick. I hoped he'd got them all right. I couldn't think about arithmetic; somebody had taken my marbles. Even if I could have thought about the sums, I still couldn't have done them. I'd rather risk getting some of them right by copying, than the beating I'd be sure to get if I did them myself and got them all wrong. When the bell went, I wandered outside and went back to the pipe to make sure.

"You want play marble Meadie?" Gary shouted.

"Me no got no marble," I answered miserably, "Somebody teif dem."

"Who teif dem?" asked Tony.

"Me no know, you jackass," I snapped at him. "If me did know who teif dem, I woulda get dem back."

This was serious. Marbles might just be bits of glass, but to us they were valuable property. I wandered disconsolately round the yard, kicking a mango seed. I had worked hard for that collection of marbles. There were only ten of them, but I'd bought four of them and won the rest with some hard fought games. I didn't have any money to buy any more, nor any chance of getting any. I was still paying off the window I broke two weeks ago, playing cricket.

I kicked my mango seed over towards the little ones' classroom where a group of girls were playing Bluebird, and as I walked past them, I noticed Audley was crouching down behind them, with Big Alex, and he was playing marbles.

"That's funny," I thought, "he didn't have any this morning." I went over for a closer look.

"What you want?" asked Audley, straightening up.

"Nuttin'," I said casually. "Where you get dem marble?"

"How you mean, where me get dem?" he said nastily. "Me buy dem, awright?"

"So wa mek you never play wid dem dis morning?" I asked suspiciously.

"Cos me never want play wid dem awright?" he snapped back.

"When me want play marble is me own business, so you watch fe you own business and me will watch mine."

I glanced down at the ring. They were my marbles, I knew. I'd spent a lot of time looking at those marbles, counting them, polishing them; I knew they were mine.

"Dem a fe me marble." I said lamely.

I knew I couldn't prove it, and he was a big liar. He came up to me really close and looked down at me.

"So wha you a say Meadie," he hissed at me. "You a say me tief you marble?"

"Yeah," I shouted. "You a liar, and a tiefing dawg. You...you..."

I stopped; this was hopeless. Tears began to prick the backs of my eyes. I turned away and pushed through the crowd of gawping girls. I couldn't win, but I'd get him one day. The others crowded round me, concerned and sympathetic, but they all agreed there was nothing any of us could do. Audley White was a law unto himself.

I didn't tell the teacher about the marbles. What was the point? You didn't tell anyway; babies told tales because they were too young to sort their own lives out.

Audley didn't care anyway. He didn't know whose marbles they were when he took them, and as far as he was concerned, they were his now. He found them, he kept them. "Finders keepers, losers weepers." We all said that, that's why we hid them so carefully in the first place.

I didn't have any choice the next day. No marbles! I headed for the tree as soon as the bell went, and was quickly joined by about six others. I felt good today; I was swinging well. I couldn't put a foot or a hand wrong. You reached a point on the climbing tree when you knew your routine backwards and everything became easy. You knew that everyone was watching you and suddenly you were a star. The better you got however, the more people wanted to have a go, and it started to get a bit crowded on the tree. Space on the branches was at a premium, and this was when it started to get dangerous. I got to the foot of the tree to begin my fourth go, when Audley pushed in behind me.

"Go on, move," he said impatiently.

"Rest yourself Audley," I muttered back at him, swinging up into the lower branches. He followed close behind; I didn't look back, but I knew he was there, right behind me. We moved up the tree slowly, our feet finding their own way into familiar clefts and spaces. The kid in front of me was a bit nervous, and he hesitated at the top, before launching himself into the void. His hand slipped, he clumsily grabbed at branches, and jerkily, with little grace and a few painful knocks, reached the ground, landing with a thump. To the jeers and mocking laughter from the others on the tree, he limped off into the yard, rubbing his bruised arms and side.

It was my turn next, and I positioned myself carefully. I was going for the big one. Missing out the first swing, and aiming for the furthest branch would make the descent more spectacular. I paused, took a breath, and just as I was about to go, Audley leaned forward and pushed me. "Go on bwoy," he growled nastily.

The push over-balanced me, and to compensate, I pushed off too hard.

In an awful split second of realisation, I knew that I wasn't going to make it to the furthest branch. I also knew that I was going to miss all the other branches as well. The ground rushed up towards me, I put out my hands to save myself and hit the ground with a crunch that I can still remember to this day. It was one of those terrible moments of your life that your memory tries to erase, but which keeps coming back to you in the middle of the night.

I rolled over, stood up, and started to walk away. I realised something was wrong when I noticed the stunned silence behind me. Nobody laughed. My hands felt numb. I tried to bring them together to rub some feeling back into them, but I couldn't bring my arms up. The top parts tried hard, but the bottom part of both arms refused to obey. I looked down to see what was wrong. Both wrists, it seemed to me, were horribly bent. The left wrist looked like an S and the right one like a U. I was horrified. I was deformed. It was at this point that I cried.

Tony and Patrick ran over, all concerned, and started to lead me gently round to the front of the school, where Miss Jenny was sitting on the veranda having her coffee and smoking a cigarette. A small crowd had gathered round us now, chattering excitedly as we shuffled slowly across the dusty yard towards the steps that led up to the house. Miss Jenny sat calmly in her rocking chair, the smoke from her cigarette swirling in coils around her white hair. The crowd fell silent at the foot of the steps. Miss Jenny removed the cigarette from her lips and leaned forward in her chair.

"What is happening here?" she asked sharply.

From the shadows of the house stepped her sister, Miss Headman, or Miss Dreadman as we called her. She stood at the top of the steps with her thin hands on her even thinner hips.

"What have I told you about disturbing us at recess?" she snapped, her pale lips pursed tightly in disapproval.

"Please Miss, Andrew Mead drop out of the tree and him hand dem bend up," said Patrick nervously pushing me forward.

I was still sobbing quietly, utterly convinced that I was crippled for life. Miss Headman took two steps forward to look at me over her glasses. She gasped, "Lord have mercy, the boy has broken both his arms."

Miss Jenny sat unmoved in the rocking chair; she sat completely still. She then leaned forward and pointed at me accusingly.

"How many times have I told you not to climb those

trees?" she said.

"You never tell me nuttin'," I sobbed.

A gasp went up from the assembled crowd. This child dared contradict Miss Jenny, but she ignored it and I was led into a side room in the house. Cool damp towels were wrapped around my wrists and my mother was sent for.

The crowd dispersed, the bell went and life carried on as normal, as if nothing had happened. I sat on my own in the room, aware of a dull ache in my wrists, but feeling a bit less miserable because at least now I couldn't see them. I didn't get much more sympathy when my mum arrived. All she said was, "It serves you right," but still, she did show some concern.

The rest of the day, and the days that followed were vague, blurred by pain and frustration. The hospital informed me that I had severe greenstick fractures to both wrists, and put both arms in plaster, up to the armpits, with a right-angled bend at the elbow. This reduced me to having to eat like a dog, with my food cut up on a plate, drink through a straw, and had the miraculous effect of improving my handwriting. Back at school, the mango tree was definitely out of bounds.

"No more climbing that mango tree, or you will get a beating you won't forget in a hurry," were the exact words Miss Jenny used.

We did as we were told and stuck to marbles. It was a bit difficult playing with both arms in plaster but I got used to it. The first few days back were a bit strange, as everybody was extremely nice to me, even Audley, but as the days wore on things began to get back to normal. Nobody said anything about the fall, but then nobody knew, except me and Audley, that it was a bit more than an accident. After three weeks I had the plaster removed and I had new ones, which only came up as far as the elbow, allowing a lot more movement, and a week later I won my first big marble from Patrick. This might not seem a very remarkable feat, and I suppose it wasn't really. Marbles were won and lost every day, but a big marble was different. Big marbles were rare. They were like diamonds. Very few people had them. Patrick had bought two at Woolworths in Montego Bay. I won it from him because he had only got one left and he owed me two, so I took this one big one instead of two little ones, although in marble currency and rarity value, it was probably worth about ten.

I loved that marble; it was old and chipped, but it was the first big marble I had ever owned and I treasured it above everything else. I used it as my taw, my playing marble. We used to play a game called Lick and Span. You took it in turns to roll your marble out, away from you, and then your opponent had to either try and hit your marble with his, in which case you paid him two, or get close enough to span the distance between the two marbles with his hand, and you would then have to play out one. You always played with your best marble, as that was the one you wanted to keep, and paid out with the others if you lost the round. Sometimes we played with ball bearings. Car ball bearings were the most popular size, similar to that of a marble, but some people had access to bigger bearings from trucks, tractors, even bulldozers. Audley played with a tractor ball bearing, which was about the size of a ping pong ball. There was an uneasy truce between me and Audley. We kept our distance and on the occasions when we played together, there was a fairly tense atmosphere. He knew, and I knew, but nobody else did that I had a score to settle.

One morning break, about a week before I was due to have the plaster removed, I found myself playing marbles with Audley out in the front yard. I was using the BIG marble and he was using a big ball bearing. It was even, hit for hit. He would win two, and I would win two back, and neither of us spoke. Break time was nearly over when Audley rolled his ball bearing towards the classroom steps to take us in the right direction for when the bell went. I casually rolled mine after his, not really concentrating, and it came to rest against a little chip of wood about eleven inches from his. I tried to span the distance, but my outstretched middle finger was a fraction away from the ball bearing. No amount of knuckle cracking or finger pulling would make any difference. All Audley had to do was roll his ball bearing gently eleven inches, and I would have to pay out two marbles. I struggled. Never mind, I'd just won two off him anyway in the last round. Audley picked up his ball bearing, but instead of rolling it gently against mine, he stretched up with his arm and threw it down with all the strength he could muster, on to my big marble.

There was a dreadful splintering crunch and all that was left of my one and only, my pride and joy, my most treasured possession, were hundreds of little pieces of glass. I couldn't believe it. I was too stunned to say anything. Audley laughed nastily, and without thinking, or caring, about the consequences, I lifted both my plastered arms and brought them together, hard, on either side of his head. Audley howled with pain and sunk to his knees clutching his crushed ears, and I looked up to see Miss Jenny standing at the top of the steps, arms folded, eyes boring straight into me.

I thoroughly deserved the beating I got, but I didn't care. I'd got my revenge and Audley White left us alone after that. He left at the end of that term and when we came back after the summer, we were the big kids. It's amazing the trouble you can get yourself into, over little bits of glass.

The Dead Tree

The moonlight turned the path into a white rib-
bon that stretched ahead in a succession of folds
and dips across the fields. It ended under the
Dead Tree, by the gate, which led to the staff houses. The
Dead Tree wasn't really dead. It was, in fact, very much
alive, a huge cotton tree which spread its twisted branches,
covered in moss and spiders' webs to create a dark pool
of shade, where people would sit and shelter from the
fierce sun.

We never sat under the Dead Tree, and no child we
knew would ever dream of sitting under the Dead Tree,

because lurking in those dark shadows, close to the cool, smooth trunk, was a grave. This grave was surrounded by an enclosure of old iron railings, and had a gate, which was rusted, shut at one end. The large tombstone marking the grave, had an angel with outstretched wings standing over it, so it always seemed as if there was someone standing there, especially at night.

My brother and I stood at the start of the path across the fields. It was always like this. Whenever we got to this point, we stopped. The path led from the school grounds to the staff cottages. We lived in the school grounds and often had to use the path to get to the staff cottages and visit friends, run errands or get to town the quick way. It was OK during the day, provided you ran past the Dead Tree holding your breath, (so you didn't breathe in the 'Duppy-ghost') but at night it required a steel will, and two of you, at the very least, to tackle the path past the Dead Tree. Still we stood there, neither of us wanting to be the first to go.

"Come on," I said. "Mek a move."

We set off together down the path, jogging gently. We were both barefoot and the slightly mossy limestone path felt good beneath our feet. We passed the stand of bamboo on our left, and the shadows flickered as the moon shone through the slender green leaves. The path dipped downwards towards the swampy ground between the two playing fields, and the big mango tree on the right cast a shadow in the moonlight. We thumped noisily across the wooden sleepers and crossed the ditch and ran up the gentle slope on the other side. We kept jogging until the fence on our left turned into a hedge; the path curved gently towards the gate and the Dead Tree was in sight. We slowed to a walk, and then, praying all the time that the gate would be off the latch, we took a deep breath and sprinted. I got to the gate first and hit it with the palm of my hand on the top bar. It was open and flew back with a bang against the railings of the grave. We shot through and kept running till we hit the tarmac outside the staff cottages where we both collapsed, panting. We lay on our backs, looking up at the sky to get our breath back.

The asphalt felt warm on the backs of my legs and shoulders, and the sky was white with stars. We'd made it! After about five minutes, we got up and wandered across to the house we'd come to visit. This was not just a social call; we'd come to do business.

Steve, my brother, was a serious collector of bubble-gum cards. I collected them too, but I lacked the optimism and patience necessary to acquire a full set. I would feel cheated when I opened a pack to find I already had three of the five cards. Steve, however, would feel elation because he had two new ones to add to his collection. Anyway, the reason we had risked our lives to pass the Dead Tree, on this particular evening, was this. Steve only needed one more to complete the full set of World War Two Cards and he had been told that this kid, Lesley Graham, had the one he wanted. We walked across the grass, up the steps and opened the screen door to the veranda at the back of the house. Stepping inside we closed the door gently behind us. Steve moved forward and knocked softly on the kitchen door. A light went on and the figure of Mrs. Graham appeared through the frosted glass. The door opened.

"Oh!" she looked surprised.

"Please Mrs. Graham," said Steve, in a meek voice. "Me can chat to Lesley please?"

"What do you want Lesley for?" Mrs. Graham asked in a frosty voice. She spoke with a posh Kingston accent. I don't think she liked us much. She was afraid that we would spoil her 'nice little pickney', even though we were white. 'After all, they run around barefoot and speak the worst patois possible, like those little black children,' I heard her tell a friend of hers one day. I couldn't understand people like her. She spent her whole life trying to behave like a white person, while I spent my whole life trying not to. Very strange!

"I want to swap some bubble-gum cards wid him Mrs. Graham," said Steve, politely. I could tell by the look on his face that the effort of being polite to this woman was nearly killing him, but he wanted that card.

"You can see him for five minutes, OK? I will fetch him, wait here."

She closed the door and her blurred back view disappeared into another room. Steve and I stood outside the door in the dark.

"I hate dat woman," said Steve in a low voice. "You see how she squeeze up her mout when she look pon you. Her face come in like fowl bot bot."

We both stifled giggles and the thought of Mrs. Graham's face looking like a chicken's bottom made me want to laugh out loud. I was just about to burst with uncontrollable laughter, when I saw her coming back with the precious Lesley behind her. The door opened, and the veranda light was switched on simultaneously. We both stood blinking in the light. Lesley stood in the doorway. His mother, hands on hips stood behind him.

"You have five minutes, do you hear? Then you are going to your bed."

She turned again and click, clicked away across the stone tiles to the next room.

Lesley had a huge wadge of cards in his hand.

"What you want swap, Meadie?" he asked. "Me tink you did got all of them."

"Me don't got the whole set yet." Steve answered truthfully.

"Me only need three more," he lied.

"Which one dem you want?" asked Lesley.

I could sense from the tone of his voice that he felt he was in a pretty powerful position. He had something that Steve wanted, and he was going to take advantage of it.

"Show me wat you got," said Steve anxiously. "I will tell you."

Lesley thumbed through the cards quickly, moving them from the top of the pile to the bottom like a gambler. Steve moved closer and looked intently at them muttering, "Got, got, got, got, got," as each successive, familiar card flashed into view. Remembering what he'd said about needing three more, he slipped a couple of 'wants' into the litany. "Got, got, got, want, got, got, got, got, want." Each time he said 'want,' Lesley would slip a wanted card between two free fingers and carry on. He was nearing the end of his pile when suddenly the precious card, the one Steve wanted, appeared on top. He couldn't contain himself any longer. "Want!" he shouted, and made a grab at it. Lesley pulled his hands away, slipped the card off the top, put it with the others, and carried on to the end of the pack. When he had finished, he put the cards down and held up the three Steve had picked, fanning them out in front of him like a poker player.

"You want swap dese tree?" he said.

"Yeah," said Steve. "You can take all a dese." He held out his pile of swaps.

"All o dem?" asked Lesley in surprise.

"Yeah, you can tek all me swaps dem, just give me dis one here." He reached forward for the one he wanted, "Ocean Going Garage."

The card showed an enormous troop and tank carrier disgorging men and tanks onto some French beach in 1944. It was a rare card. I had never seen it before and I moved forward for a closer look. Suddenly Lesley snatched the cards away and held them up over his head.

"No!" he snapped sulkily.

"I don't want to swap nuttin'."

"Please, I beg you," implored Steve. "I will give you five shillings fe it."

"No!" said Lesley, and a stupid smile began to play around his lips, as he realised the extent of his power.

"I will give you twenty marble, all a me swap dem and I will pay you five shillings fe it. I beg you, please."

I kept out of it; I could tell Steve was getting desperate. For a start, he didn't have twenty marbles, and he didn't have five pennies, let alone five shillings.

Lesley had moved back into the kitchen by now, still holding the cards over his head and Steve was still standing on the top step, pleading with him. Their voices were getting louder and louder, and I knew that Mrs. Graham would come out any minute, and that would be that. At that moment, Lesley said, "Alright, alright." He brought the cards down, and held them with both hands, in front of him. "You really want dese cards?" he asked. "You can tek dem."

And with that, he brought the cards up in front of his face, ripped them in half, and threw them on the floor. There was an awful silence. Steve looked down at the torn cards and then up at Lesley who stood with a stupid lop-sided grin of triumph on his face.

That was it. Steve cracked. He hurled himself in fury at Lesley, throwing him back against the kitchen cabinets, which rocked violently, but luckily, did not fall.

"Leave him Steve," I hissed as loudly as I dared, and reached forward to grab him by the collar and drag him off. Lesley was cowering on the floor by the cabinet, snivelling, when Mrs. Graham came in.

"Get out of my kitchen!" she yelled.

I retreated, dragging Steve with me. He wasn't saying anything, but tears of rage were running down his face.

38

"How dare you come in my house and behave like that? I am going to speak to your father in the morning."
We stumbled out the door and down the steps. The screen door slammed behind us, and Mrs. Graham shut the kitchen door so hard the whole house shook.

Steve set off at a run in the direction of home, still crying with rage and frustration, and muttering threats against Lesley Graham and his mother. I followed. I kept thinking about what had just happened and I couldn't work it out. There was a lot of things that people said and did that I couldn't work out.

We got into a lot of trouble over that night. Mrs. Graham saw dad the next day and we had to go and see him in his study that evening. I told Steve to keep his mouth shut, and I explained exactly what had happened. Dad understood. He said something about Lesley being an only child and a bit spoilt and added something about Mrs. Graham that I didn't hear. I don't think he liked her either. Steve had to apologise to her, and to Lesley, which he just about managed, and that evening in bed, we plotted revenge.

The next day we came home from school the quick way. As we passed the Dead Tree, we slowed right down and looked up at the branches, checked the position of the bushes on either side of the path, and made some mental notes. Once home, we searched the yard for a length of rope and some suitable sticks or poles. The rope we found behind the groundsman's shed, and we took the poles from the school garden. Steve rummaged around in the bottom of dad's wardrobe and found an old black jacket, while I was fortunate to find a slightly rotting breadfruit in the rubbish bin outside our kitchen. We took our equipment into the far outhouse that we used as a den, and set to work. We tied the sticks together in the shape of a cross, leaving a considerable amount of rope hanging loose. Next we stuck the breadfruit on the top and hung the jacket over the crosspiece. What we ended up with was a scarecrow with a lengthy piece of rope attached. We hid the 'body' under the bench, covered with old newspapers, and for the next few days, we bided our time.

We were waiting for two things. Firstly, darkness – the moon was full, which was no good. Secondly, Lesley Graham and his mother had to come out at night and walk past the Dead Tree. This did not happen very often as Mrs. Graham rarely ventured out in the evening, and of course, precious Lesley was certainly not allowed out on his own. However, as luck would have it, our chance came just eight days later. By this time, the moon had waned and was only a sliver of silver in the sky, and we knew that Lesley's father was going to be working late at school that night. Whenever Mr. Graham worked late, preparing or marking examination papers, Mrs. Graham would bring him a meal. We knew what time he had his meal in the chemistry lab because we knew everything that went on in the school, after dark, and at weekends. We also knew that when Mrs. Graham walked up to school with her husband's meal, Lesley always went with her.

We set off down the path that evening with about twenty minutes in which to prepare everything. We were taking a big risk as we knew we had to wait in the bushes, just a few feet away from the grave under the Dead Tree, for about five minutes. It was pitch black when we got there for night had well and truly fallen. Steeling ourselves we lifted the 'body' over the railings and stood him up behind the angel. Then I threw the end of the rope over the branch, which grew across the grave. It took three attempts to get it over without catching on any smaller branches. I then tied the rope tightly round my wrist, so I didn't lose it, and crossed the path to hide in the bushes.

Steve crouched down behind the grave and with our hearts pounding with fear and excitement, we waited.

The night was very still. The crickets chirruped merrily in the bushes, but otherwise there was no sound. I squatted down, keeping the rope taut, and peered through the blackness to the other side of the path. I couldn't see Steve – he was behind one of the buttress roots of the tree, well hidden from view. I looked beyond the gate to the staff cottages, which were all dark except for the flicker of an oil lamp from the kitchen window of the Graham's house. There must have been a power cut, I thought to myself. No big deal; we were always having power cuts, especially in the early evening when everyone got home and turned their lights and radios on.

The minutes seemed to drag and I was beginning to get jittery. I'd never stayed this long by the Dead Tree before. I turned and looked back towards the school when my blood turned to ice and my heart literally stopped beating. About 100 yards away, five feet off the ground was a small red light, which occasionally glowed brighter, and it was coming towards us. It wasn't moving very quickly and I couldn't take my eyes off it. "Rolling Calf!" The words slammed into my consciousness. I'd heard these stories about the Rolling Calf, a calf's head with fiery eyes that floated around, dragging chains behind it. I couldn't hear any chains, and this one had only one eye, but I was certain that that was what it was. I heard a warning whistle from the other side of the path. "Dem a come. Dem a come."

I dragged my eyes away from the Rolling Calf, to the gate. Lesley and his mother were approaching fast, Mrs. Graham striding quickly with an aluminium lunch pail in one hand and a hurricane lamp in the other. Lesley scurried along behind her, trying to keep up. I looked back to the red light, which was nearly upon me, when

41

suddenly, my nerve broke. I couldn't go up the path, I couldn't go through the gate, so I jumped out across the path meaning to grab Steve, and run across the fields, to the small grove of guava trees on the other side. The problem was that in my panic I'd forgotten the rope, hooked tight around my wrist. It jerked me back and I slipped, sat down heavily in the middle of the path while the 'body' on the other end of the rope, shot up soundlessly from behind the grave, just as Mrs. Graham and Lesley reached the gate. Mrs. Graham dropped the hurricane lamp and the lunch pail. The scream she let out was equal to the yell of terror from my left. The red light shot through the air, landed in my lap, and began to burn a hole in my trousers. There was the sound of running feet in both directions, and I sat there in a state of numbed shock. The smell of cigarette smoke, scorching material and paraffin from the lamp brought me back to my senses. As the noises of fear faded, I scrambled to my feet, brushing the cigarette end off my shorts, and disentangled myself from the rope around my wrist.

Steve came stumbling towards me from the shadows by the grave, doubled up with suppressed laughter, incapable of speech. I was still too dazed with shock to laugh. I walked nervously across the grave and reached over the railings for the 'body'. I pulled it roughly over the spikes, wrapping the rope quickly and untidily around it. Steve started slapping me on the back, barely able to speak with laughter.

"We ketch two a dem!" he spluttered. "You see de guy wid de cigarette? Him run like a dawg and Lesley, and 'im mada. Dem foot never touch ground."

I laughed nervously. Steve had obviously realised what that red light was. I wasn't going to tell him that I'd been as scared as they were. I was glad it was dark and he couldn't see my face.

"Come on." I muttered. "We better move. If somebody ketch we, we dead."

At that moment, I heard a faint shuffling sound from the shadows under the tree. We both froze. Steve suddenly stopped laughing, as if he'd been switched off, and out of the silence, came a deep, low chuckle. "Ha ha ha ha." The hairs on the back of my neck stood up, and for the second time that night, my blood ran cold.

"Run!" I yelled, and we did, in blind panic, stumbling over the rough ground and tripping on the rope. We didn't stop till we collapsed in a heap on the back veranda.

I slept badly that night. I kept hearing that awful laugh from the grave. Nobody ever knew it was us who had nearly scared Mrs. Graham out of her mind. She was in bed for a week, and she never went up that path at night again. Neither did I – I always went the long way round. In fact, it was months before Steve or I went past the grave again in the daytime, let alone at night, and we never told anybody about what we'd done. We were too scared.

We had thought we were so clever, but that duppy of the Dead Tree, he had the last laugh.

Cookie's Knife

Old man Burkett, whose land was behind our school, took it into his head one year to plough up the field adjoining our school yard. We watched with bored fascination as the ancient tractor trundled up and down, throwing up clouds of choking dust that settled over everything like brown talcum powder. Our boredom and indifference, however, turned to joyful, mouth-watering anticipation, when we realised that he was planting sugar-cane. We watched with delight as the curious little sticks of cane that had been stuck haphazardly in drunken rows across the field, shot up into elegant waving green leaves that promised a feast of sweet delights for little boys. It was separated from us by a three-strand barbed wire fence... not enough.

We were strictly forbidden to enter the canefield.

"You will not go into Mr. Burkett's canefield."

"No Miss Jenny." We all chorused, and promptly set about making a large gap in the barbed wire behind the largest of two logwood trees, that acted as fence posts and were out of sight of the house. There were four of us that did the work involved in making the gap big enough to get through completely unseen, and as quickly as possible both ways. The little ones were kept well away with threats, and in some cases, promises of mint balls and grater cake, and when the job had been done, we shifted large amounts of banana leaves and cane trash, into the gap between the bushes and the trees, so that it was invisible to the casual observer. We then disappeared into the canefield at breaktime and lunchtime, and lost ourselves in the cool, rustling forest of canes, making sure that we went right to the middle of the field, before we started trying to help ourselves to sticks of sugar-cane, – fat, swollen and full of juice as only fresh cut cane can be.

After these first expeditions to the heart of the cane forest, we discovered that cane is extremely hard to break. We came away empty handed, leaving behind several broken plants which we had all stamped on and kicked violently in our frustration.

What we needed was a decent knife, and Tony knew where to get one.

"Cookie got one big ole knife, sit down pon top a de fire," he said. "I never see she use it. It always sit down in de same place."

"Who a go tek it den?" I asked looking round at the other three in turn.

"You can do it," said Desmond raising his good arm and

poking me in the chest. "She like you Meadie 'cos you is a likkle white boy."

"Hush you mout Dundus boy," I snapped back at him.

"Why you no do it, what happen, you 'fraid?"

"No me no 'fraid," said Desmond. "You tink me 'fraid? Right, you watch me."

And so it was, that after school that afternoon, while the rest of us gathered round Cookie's kitchen door, begging johnny cakes and peg bread, Desmond sneaked in the opening at the back, and silently removed Cookie's old knife from the fireplace. We hung around outside for a few minutes making sure that she hadn't missed it, and when, after about five minutes we heard her start singing 'Rock of Ages' and banging a few pans about, we fled down to the end of the yard to find Desmond. He was waiting behind the tree, a smug grin of triumph on his face.

"Who say me 'fraid – you wouldn't do it. See it here, how much you a go gi me fe it?" he said, sitting with his back against the tree and dangling the knife enticingly in front of us.

"Gi you?" said Tony. "How you mean, gi you? You never say we ha fi gi you nuttin'."

"Well me a say you ha fi gi me something now, aw right?" Desmond sneered.

He was like that, Desmond. One minute he was one of you, on your side, your friend, and the next minute he would turn and disown you or refuse to co-operate. I suppose he did put up with a lot. Because he'd had Polio when he was a baby, he'd got one withered arm and a leg that didn't work as well as the other healthy one, so the big kids used to call him 'withered hand' and 'peg leg'. There was this one really big boy called Anthony Wallis who used to treat him like he was his servant, making him fetch things for him, taking his marbles and kicking him around all the time.

"Nobody goin' gi you nuttin' fe dat knife Desmond." I snarled at him. "Dat knife a fe all o we."

"Dat knife a fe all o we," he mimicked back at me in a singsong, whining voice.

"Hear dis bwoy, dis knife belong to I; I tief it, I keep it, right?" He held the knife in his good right hand and stood up, awkwardly backing away from us towards the canefield, the knife behind his back. None of us wanted to tackle him, not while he had the knife, and anyway, Desmond was really strong even if he did only have one arm that worked. Nobody spoke and Desmond stopped backing away and stood, head slightly forward, his useless left arm hanging loosely at his side, all his weight on his good right leg. His eyes narrowed and he slowly brought the knife round from behind his back and pointed it at us.

"You want dis knife?" he said slowly. "You gi me one shillin' fe it. You hear dat, one shillin'."

"One shillin'?" retorted Patrick contemptuously, speaking for the first time. "One kick in a you backside, one lick in a you big ugly mout."

Patrick moved menacingly towards him and Desmond raised the knife and held it in front of him, inches from Patrick's face. Patrick stopped and glared at Desmond; his raised hands, bunched into fists, fell hopelessly by his side. He turned to us, shrugging his shoulders, palms out-stretched.

"Wha wrong wid him?"

"Nuttin' wrong wid me," said Desmond. "I tek a risk, you pay me. What wrong wid dat?"

"Leave him." I said. "Him mad."

I turned and pushed my way back through the gap in the fence and Tony and Patrick followed, leaving Desmond standing there, the knife still pointed towards us.

"One shillin'!" we heard him shout.

"Don't bother wid him," said Tony. "Tomorrow will be different. Him will gi we the knife tomorrow."

But tomorrow was not any different. It was Friday. We did not see Desmond till nearly lunchtime because he was late for school, not arriving until eleven thirty. He avoided looking at any of us, and sat at his desk near the back, on his own, his head down over his book, copying verses from the Bible laboriously, tongue protruding from the side of his mouth in fierce concentration. When the bell went, we all stood behind our desks automatically, hands together and eyes closed, while Miss Jenny stood before us and we said Grace as we did every day.

"For what we are about to receive may the Lord make us truly thankful. Amen."

We raised our heads and stood silently, arms by our sides, not moving a muscle. Miss Jenny looked up and fixed us with her grey eyes, not speaking for what seemed like hours, and when she did speak, her voice cut the expectant silence like the proverbial knife.

"Would the three boys at the back wait behind. I would like to speak with them."

She needed no names; we knew who we were; you couldn't get any further back than me, Patrick and Tony. I went hot and there was a tight feeling in my stomach, like someone was squeezing my intestines into a little ball. The girls filed out silently into the yard, followed by the boys. Desmond was the last to go, and as he walked past the window, he looked up, and there was a look on his face of triumphant delight. Miss Jenny wanted us, not him, and he knew why.

My mouth was dry and I was beginning to sweat more

than usual, big drops running down my neck and down the back of my shirt making me feel extremely uncomfortable. Miss Jenny was a formidable character. She was no more than about five foot two and slightly built, but she held herself erect and always dressed in very long skirts and high collared blouses, rather Victorian in appearance. She had white hair, which was always swept back into a tight plait, which hung down her back, almost to her waist. She had a very pale complexion and grey eyes, which looked right into you and made you feel really guilty even when you hadn't done anything. For an old lady, (she must have been ninety), she was incredibly strong and could move very quickly when she wanted to.

"You three boys come to the front," she said, and we moved slowly out from behind the low wooden desks, stumbling over the cast iron feet and each other. We shuffled forward rather reluctantly, and stood in a ragged line, looking down at the dusty wooden floor. Still she did not speak, and a drop of sweat dripped off the end of my nose and landed in the dust, sending little splashes of liquid onto the toes of her immaculately polished shoes.

At last she spoke. "Desmond's mother came to see me this morning," she said, "and I am very surprised at what she told me."
She paused, letting her words sink in. Patrick shuffled his feet.

"Keep still Patrick White," she snapped, "or you will feel my strap across your backside sooner than you think."

We all froze, hardly daring to breathe. We all feared Miss Jenny's strap. It was black and menacing like a barber's leather strap and it lay in the narrow trough at the front of her desk, inches from our noses. All of us had felt it at some time or other; 'The Black Spider!' It was legendary. A big boy called Alex had hidden it once under the floorboards of the little ones' classroom, but it had been found. No one ever knew how, and he had been given fifteen of the best in front of the whole school. Miss Jenny spoke again, quietly this time, but with a hard steely edge to her voice.

"As I was saying, Mrs Parsons spoke with me this morning, and it seems that you boys have been making Desmond's life a misery, laughing at him and teasing him, and that is something that I will not tolerate."

I was so surprised at what she said I opened my mouth to say something but thought better of it and closed it again. This wonderful sense of relief flooded over me. It wasn't the knife as she didn't know about the knife. This was bad enough but we'd had this before. Desmond was always blaming us for what the big ones did to him. I suppose it was because he knew he couldn't tell on them being afraid of what they'd do to him. He had to take his frustration and anger out on somebody, so he told on us, his friends. That's what friends are for, I guess.

As I said before, he was really a strange boy. My thoughts were interrupted by Miss Jenny's voice again.

"You should not mock the afflicted, do you hear me?"

"Yes, Miss Jenny," we mumbled looking at the floor.

"Look at me when you are speaking to me." she snapped. "Do you hear me?"

We raised our heads in unison and chorused, "Yes, Miss Jenny."

We kept our heads up and I tried desperately to avoid looking at her eyes. I was convinced that if she looked into my eyes she would see right into my head and know what I was thinking. I knew what was coming next; we'd had it before. She made us hold out our hands and we got three each with the end of the strap, three stinging lashes that made the tears prickle and burn the insides of your eyes and your hand felt as if it had been branded with a hot poker. Then we had to stay in, miss our lunch and write, 'I must not mock the afflicted' two hundred times. Miss Jenny sat at her desk and Cookie came in with a cloth and Miss Jenny's dinner on a tray.

She looked at us and shook her head sadly, "Dem not so bad Miss. Jenny." she said. "Dem not so bad, is the devil mek dem do it. I will pray for dem," and out she went tut-tutting softly, still shaking her head.

The rest of the lunch hour passed slowly in the small wooden classroom. The only sounds were the scratch of pens on paper, the interminable tick of the big clock on the wall and the sound of Miss Jenny's cutlery clinking on china. From outside came the shouts and laughter of the others at play, taunting us with their freedom. I longed to be outside, to feel the sun on my face, to run through the grass, swing in the trees, or lie in the canefield and look up at the sky through the sharp green leaves. Instead we were kept in again, writing lines again, and it was Desmond's fault, again.

When the bell went Miss Jenny stood up, stepped forward and took the paper from the desks in front of us. "Stay away from Desmond Parsons," she warned, then turned and strode out of the room.

The rest of the class pushed in silently, followed by Miss Miller, the afternoon teacher. We then spent the next hour being hit and yelled at for failing to understand the rudiments of long multiplication. When at last the bell went for afternoon break, we exploded into the yard, drank long and greedily from the tap, and for a few moments, just savoured the sheer pleasure of being outside again. Desmond was nowhere to be seen and we did as we were told for once. We left him alone. I knew what the other two were thinking but none of us said anything.

Patrick found an old piece of rope, discarded by the girls as too short for skipping, and we started playing high jump in the front yard, taking it in turns to hold the rope, while the other one tried to jump it. It was Tony's turn to jump and Patrick and I were holding the rope when suddenly, seemingly from out of nowhere came Desmond. He was charging towards the rope, obviously intent on jumping it, his useless left arm flapping at his side. He had this wild look on his face and his mouth was twisted into a grimace of angry determination. He took off about three feet away from the rope, trying to pull his weak leg up out of the way. For what seemed like a long time, he hung in the air and would have cleared it easily if Patrick and I, as if we'd been given a signal, had not suddenly jerked the rope upwards, caught his bad leg, and tipped his face forwards towards the ground.

Desmond hit the dirt with a terrible crunch; he'd tried to save himself but only having one good arm made it difficult. He turned his head to the side to try and save his face but he landed flat, his stomach and the side of his face hitting the ground simultaneously, sending up a cloud of dust. The yard went silent. There was something about the way his body hit the ground that made us realise he was hurt. Nobody moved. We all stood there, like we were in a photograph, waiting for Desmond to move, but he didn't. As I stood completely still, watching him lying there, I suddenly felt really sorry for him. This great wave of pity welled up inside me and I felt so sad for him. He couldn't help having a withered arm and leg, and yet he was teased and abused. Nobody wanted him on their team because he couldn't hold the bat properly, and he couldn't run fast enough or climb as high as everyone else. It wasn't surprising he was always so angry, aggressive and vindictive. Again, as if we'd been given a signal, Patrick and I rushed forward and knelt down beside him.

"Desmond, Desmond git up," Patrick gasped helplessly.

He still did not move. He was breathing in short gasps and the saliva was running out of his mouth onto the dirt. "Tek him inside," I said and tried to lift him by the arm. He was a dead weight. Between us, Patrick and I managed to drag him across the yard and up the steps into the classroom. Someone had sent for Miss Jenny and she pulled forward her chair from behind her desk and we dumped him in it. The rest of the school were either on the steps peering in through the door, or gathered around every available window, staring in morbid fascination. Desmond sat in the chair, his head lolling forward onto his chest, while Miss Jenny wiped his face and mouth with a wet flannel. Gradually he appeared to regain control of his head and he lifted it up and opened his eyes. Suddenly, without warning his whole body threw itself forward and he was violently and spectacularly sick, all over the front three rows of desks.

If the last five minutes had seemed like slow motion, the rest of the afternoon was a blur. Desmond was taken home, our class had to spend the rest of the afternoon outside under the mango tree while the classroom was cleaned, and Patrick and I got a real beating. The full length of the strap, on backsides and legs, our heads held tightly under Miss Jenny's arm. I told you she was really strong for an old lady. Needless to say, I got another walloping when I got home and spent the weekend in disgrace. No pocket money, no play, no nothing. Only extra washing up and early to bed. The only thing that kept me moderately cheerful was the thought that, by Monday, Desmond would have forgotten everything that had happened, we'd have the knife and we would have as much cane as we wanted. He was like that, Desmond, like I said before.

I got to school early on Monday. I waited for Patrick outside his dad's garage and we ran together, through the

Texaco station and down George Street, narrowly avoiding being run over by a tractor coming out of Old Burkett's front gate. What was that doing there? Desmond was waiting like I knew he would be, by the school gate. Tony, who came from the opposite direction to us, arrived panting and sweating; it was nearly 8.30 and the sun was already really hot.

"You got de knife?" he asked breathlessly.

"Right here," replied Desmond, patting the front of his shirt so we could see the shape of the handle pressing against the khaki.

"Come, we go cut some cane."

We walked nonchalantly past the house, round the classroom and were preparing for the sprint down the backyard when, as we came around the corner of Cookie's kitchen, we all four stopped dead in utter dismay and disbelief. It was gone, the field was empty. Old Burkett had had it cut over the weekend, and not a stick was left. Desmond swore loudly, and taking the knife out of the front of his shirt, he ran down the yard and threw it as hard as he could. It sailed up in a high graceful arc, and we all watched as it landed in a pile of cane trash in the middle of the field. I remember thinking "that's what that tractor was doing coming out of Burkett's gate." I looked at Tony and Patrick and they looked at me. We didn't say anything. Patrick spat viciously and turned and walked back to the classroom. Tony and I turned to follow him, leaving Desmond still standing staring at the empty field.

"Too much cane mek you teeth rotten," he said. I just laughed. You have to really; otherwise you'd cry.

The River

A bicycle was a luxury. Adults owned bikes, and went to work on them. Kids like us rode bikes that were past their usefulness to adults but they were very hard to come by. We had one which we shared among the four of us, which worked alright until we all wanted to go to the same place at the same time. Then it started getting illegal. Four on a bike is just about the limit if you want to travel in reasonable comfort, and we only got caught once, when a police Landrover came up on us from behind. Kids were flying off that bike like chickens with a mongoose after them. The bike hit the asphalt with me still on it, as I was doing the pedalling. I tried to scramble up, out of the road but the policeman grabbed me by the back of my shirt and lifted me off the ground. My legs were still trying to follow the others through the fence, and into the canefield, so I looked like one of those cartoon characters running in mid air.

"You want me lock you up bwoy?" he growled at me. He swung me round and thumped me down in front of him, transferring his grip to the front of my shirt.

"No sah," I stammered. I didn't recognise this policeman and he didn't know me, it was obvious, as he would have made some comment about telling my dad by now.

"If I ketch the four o' you on dat cycle again you will go to court, you hear me?"

"Yes sah," I croaked, my throat feeling dry and tight.

"You tink jus because you is a white bwoy, you can do what you want?"

I just looked at him with narrowed eyes. I hated people calling me 'white boy'. I wasn't any colour, I was just a boy, so was everybody else. The policeman looked beyond me in the vain hope of catching sight of the others.

"Tell them other pickney that I will lock them up if I catch dem."

He let go of my shirt and pushed me away from him. I stumbled backwards over the bike and he turned on his heels, squeezed back into the Landrover and raced off in a haze of petrol fumes. I was left sitting on the road, on top of the bicycle, with a brake lever sticking in my backside. I picked myself up, as the others appeared out of the sugarfield, laughing.

"You want me lock you up bwoy!" said Boysie in a deep voice, imitating the policeman.

"Hush you mout Boysie," I laughed back.

"What did happen to you den, you run like dawg when you see the Babylon?"

"You want to know why we run?" asked Boysie.

"Is cos me know that policeman. Im is my auntie sister cousin, im come from Black River and im is a wicked man. You lucky de res a we run Jobe, cos if im did ketch all o we, im would a lock we up fe true."

"You want we walk now den?" I asked meekly.

"No." said Maxie. "Ride de bicycle, you tink we 'fraid o no Babylon?"

Buoyed up by the defiant note in Maxie's voice, we all piled back onto the bike and set off. Boysie was pedalling this time. Maxie, being the smallest sat on the crossbar, John, the next up in size sat on the handlebars, as I stood on the wheelnuts of the back wheel holding on to Boysie's shoulders. Progress was slow but steady, and it was certainly quicker than walking.

After another two miles we turned off the main road, and onto the farm path that led across the fields to the river. It ran through private farmland that belonged to an extremely rich white man, whose wife was a friend of my mum's. We had an open invitation to swim there whenever we wanted. The last mile was across fields, which meant throwing the bike over the fence, running through the long grass that grew down to the river's edge, and eventually clambering over the wall and into the small picnic area under the trees, where we used to swim. The river widened into a deep pool at this point, and was crossed by an old hump-backed stone bridge. About thirty yards downstream from the bridge, a wooden boom was set into the rock on either bank and enclosed the swimming area.

We had run the last mile across the fields, and arriving hot and sweating, we tore off our clothes and, clambering up on to the stone parapet of the bridge, dived into the cool, clear, glass green water. The sensation of hitting the water, and the taste and feel of it, was indescribable. I pulled out of the dive quickly to avoid hitting the bottom, and swam under water until I reached the bottom. I came up for air, gasping and laughing with the sheer pleasure of being alive. The river was like a little piece of paradise on earth, and I loved it.

The others were in the water by now, having jumped or dived off the bridge but Boysie stood on the bank, looking apprehensive and watching us with envy. He couldn't swim. Not a stroke. We had all tried to teach him, in the sea, where it was easy, but he just couldn't do it. He was really scared of the water, but at the same time he loved the idea of being in it and swimming.

Close to the bank there was a narrow shelf of sand and rock about a metre wide, where Boysie stood, up to his waist in the water, while the rest of us dive-bombed off the bridge, and had races up and down the pool.

After about half an hour of this, three of us came out of the water and sat in the shade, talking and laughing, while Boysie stayed in the water, splashing and grabbing at the crayfish that darted in and out of the holes in the bank.

About a month before I thought my end had come trying to catch these crayfish. I dived down to a somewhat large hole about six feet under, pushed my hand in and grabbed this big crayfish by the tail. When I tried to pull my hand out, it was stuck. I panicked. My life flashed in front of my eyes and I kept seeing this newspaper headline:-

BOY DROWNS CATCHING CRAYFISH

Just as my lungs were about to burst, and death was staring me in the face, the thought occurred to me that it might be a good idea to let go of the crayfish. I did, and my hand slid easily out of the hole and I shot to the surface like a cork out of a bottle. Another headline flashed in my mind's eye:-

GREEDY BOY NEARLY
DROWNS CATCHING CRAYFISH

There was no chance of Boysie drowning; he never put his face anywhere near the water, let alone in it.

It was a Saturday afternoon, the sun was warm, the sky was blue, the water was cool and it was quiet and peaceful. I stretched out on the bench, enjoying the warmth and stillness, when I had this strange sensation that all was not well. It was too quiet, there was something missing. I turned towards the river and an icy claw gabbed at my chest and throat so I could barely speak. "Where Boysie gone?" I croaked, but straight away I knew the answer. He'd fallen off the ledge into the deep water. Some instinct made me jump up onto the bench and look downstream. I saw Boysie's head break the surface about forty metres away. "See im deh," I yelled in panic and leapt across the grass and into the water, with my eyes on the spot where I had last seen him. The others followed. Once again the headlines flashed through my head:-

BOY DROWNS WHILE SWIMMING! MOTHER MOURNS DEAD SON.

It had rained a lot in the last four weeks and the river was deep and flowing pretty rapidly. In a few strokes, carried along by the current, I reached the place where I'd seen Boysie last. He'd been swept further downstream and I saw his arm and head about twenty metres away, closer to the bank. I swam towards him, and luckily he'd got tangled in some weeds which held him there. As I got closer, I dived, came up underneath him, and with one huge effort, pushed him out of the water and into the mud and vegetation at the side of the river.

He lay on his side, on top of the broad leaves of the dashine that grew by the water's edge, and I scrambled up beside him. The others had arrived by this time and between us we managed to drag him across the mud and through the huge umbrella-like leaves, to firmer ground, our feet sinking up to our knees in the sucking, black mud. Boysie lay, not moving, on the spiky grass, and the three of us stood around him, covered in mud, looking like creatures from the black lagoon. John's voice was squeaky with shock, "Kiss me neck Jobe, im dead." He did look dead. He was completely still. I knelt beside him and shook him. "Boysie! Boysie, wake up!" The headlines began to flash again:-

SCHOOL BOY DROWNING HORROR
RIVER DEATH

A serious panic began to grip me. The other two just stood there, too numbed by shock to say anything. I jumped up and grabbed Maxie by the shoulders.
"Wha we a go do man, de bwoy dead, we ha fe find somebody."
"You go Jobe, run!"
Run? Where to? Nobody lived round here; it was just fields full of cows, and an airstrip where little planes full of ganja would fly secretly to Miami. I started running towards the road. I ran with that desperate feeling of panic blinding me to the pain of the rough, uneven grass and the patches of stones. I didn't know what I'd do when I got to the road. What do you do when your friend has just drowned?

I reached the fence and rolled underneath it, catching my back on the barbed wire and scraping my arms and knees on the sharp stones at the side of the track. I scrambled to my feet and kept running. I was breathing heavily now and the blood was pounding through my head. "Find somebody! Find somebody! Find somebody!" The farm track seemed to stretch endlessly away from me, I wished I'd brought the bike, but it would have delayed me across the field.

I didn't remember it being this far to the road. I tripped and stumbled forward onto the stones, scraping my stomach badly in the fall. I kept going. My head, still pounding, began to clear a bit, and disturbing thoughts invaded my brain. I imagined Boysie's auntie, and his grandmother, sitting in their little house with tears running down their faces, as I told them about the accident. It suddenly began to dawn on me that it was my responsibility, my fault he was dead. I had taken him swimming; the river was a dangerous place for a non-swimmer. It was my fault. I would be charged, taken to court, locked up. I began to slow down. I didn't want to reach the road. All I wanted to do was run away and hide. I couldn't face what was going to happen. I wanted to turn the clock back an hour, two hours. Maybe it would have been better if the police had caught all of us and locked us up; at least Boysie would still be alive. The urgency went out of my running, I slowed right down to walking pace, and before I could do anything about it, I was at the road. I stood there and a large white Mercedes swept past, the occupants staring at me in disbelief. Then an old pick-up shot past, in the opposite direction, with a gang of boys in the back, who all started laughing and calling out to me as I stood miserably at the side of the road. I looked down at myself and suddenly realised that I did look very odd indeed. I was a white boy, with black mud-coated legs, covered in blood and scratches, standing by the side of the road in swimming trunks, in the middle of nowhere. For about two minutes, I didn't move and nothing came past. I eventually sat down on the grass, at the side of the road, and with a head and heart full of terrifying thoughts and feelings, began to cry.

I ignored the sound of an approaching vehicle, and sat there with my head in my hands, as it slowed down and crunched to a halt in front of me. I didn't even look up as the door slammed, and a voice broke through my pathetic cocoon of self-pity.

"What you doing here bwoy?"
I still didn't look up, but I recognised the voice. I'd heard it before, and suddenly, with a sickening thud of realisation I remembered where. I looked up slowly, and there, standing in front of me, hands on hips and a scowl all over his face was, the policeman. What could I do? I couldn't run, I couldn't lie my way out of this, I had to tell him. I staggered to my feet.

"AAAA bwoy drownded sah," I stammered pathetically. "Im drop in the river and drownded."

The policeman looked at me in disbelief. "What you mean drownded, im dead?"

"Yes sah, im look dead sah, im not moving and im look really dead sah!"

"What you mean, im look dead," snapped the policeman. "Either im dead or im alive, where is he den?"

"Down de river sah, you better come look, me will show you."

He reached out and pulled me across to the Landrover and bundled me into the back.

I sat dejected on the hard bench in the gloom, as we bumped off down the track towards the river. The policeman swung round and glared at me.

"What you doing down here. Dis is private land you know bwoy. If Missah Clark ketch you down here you are in serious trouble, you know dat?"

"Me mother know Missah Clark sah, im know say we down here."

He grunted in disgust and turned back to look at the track. "Missah Clark know say you got all dese other pickney down here?" he asked sneeringly. "Missah Clark don't want all dese people on his land."

I didn't answer. What did he mean, "dese people." They were my friends; if it was alright for me, it was alright for them. What did it matter to him anyway, it wasn't his business. I hated this policeman. I hated his disapproval of me mixing with kids who were the same colour as him, but who he regarded as inferior because they were black and poor, yet because they were with me, had access to a privilege that he didn't. Not for the first time I felt conspicuous and ashamed of my whiteness. It set me apart from my friends and made me in other people's eyes, something I didn't want to be, just another white boy.

We reached the end of the track; he stopped the Landrover and motioned to me to get out. I crawled under the fence and began to walk across the field towards the river. He had to climb the fence, which was difficult, as he was a big guy. I could hear him swearing quietly and turned to see him slip, catching his leg on the barbed wire and tearing his trousers. He swore again, loudly, and shouted at me, "Wait bwoy."

"Mek haste sah, we soon reach," I shouted back, and started running.

I could hear him start running behind me and I went faster, leaping over the mounds of grass and piles of cow mess. He came panting and stumbling after me, cursing and grunting like an angry bull. As I got closer to the river I started shouting, "John! Maxie!" but there was no reply. There was an ominous silence and I realised with growing concern that they had gone. But where? How could they have moved Boysie, and why? The policeman was quite a long way behind me now, and he had stopped running, and was picking his way through the long grass.

I looked round and called again, "Maxie! John! Whe you gone?" when I heard a hoarse, half-whispered shout from the direction of the picnic area.

"Jobe, see we here, mek haste."

Maxie's head was just visible above the low wall and he was beckoning me furiously. I looked back at the policeman who was getting closer, but was still quite a way off and trying to avoid the cows' mess which he had already got all over his boots. I ducked down in the badu leaves, ran to the wall, leapt over it and landed in a heap on the other side. I started to get up when arms dragged me down, and a hand went over my mouth.

"Hush your mouth Jobe," hissed a voice which I recognised as John's and then, "If dat Babylon ketch we, we dead."

"Boysie!" I gasped, struggling to get up, "How come...?"
The hands clamped over my mouth again, and I was dragged back into a tangled mass of bushes and weeds by the wall, and we lay there absolutely still. We could hear

the policeman in the field. He had stopped at the last place he had seen me and was obviously completely baffled.

"Where you gone bwoy?" he shouted.

We froze, eyes shut, holding our breath.

"If I ketch you, BWOY, I goin' give you good beatin'." We heard his heavy footsteps approach the wall, and stop as he looked over. I raised my head, and saw the bicycle and our clothes which had been dragged into the bushes close by us.

We heard him start to climb up onto the low wall. He lost his footing, swore loudly, and obviously gave up trying to climb over. After about two or three minutes of stomping around yelling blood-curdling threats, we heard him stomp across the field, away from us, back towards the track. We crawled out of the bushes and peered cautiously over the wall. He was halfway across the field, still muttering and swearing, and every so often he would stop, look round, and scratch his head in disbelief. We stayed crouched behind the wall until he had disappeared from sight, and then we started to laugh. I don't think I have ever felt such an overwhelming sense of relief, and joy. Boysie was alive!

I jumped on him and sat on his chest.

"Me tink you dead bwoy!!"

He pushed me off and sat up, "Yeah me dead Jobe. Me is a duppy, me a go suck out you brain through your earhole. You save me life man."

We sat and looked at each other.

"Dat Babylon never goin' to forget dis day," declared Maxie. "Nobody goin' believe 'im neither," laughed John. "De whole a Black River a go tink 'im mad!"

We laughed uncontrollably, rolling round on the ground, slapping each other on the back and wiping tears from our faces. It was indeed good to be alive.